Oh No, It's Waylon's Birthday!

by James Stevenson

Greenwillow Books, New York

Watercolor paints and a black pen were used for
the full-color art. The text type is ITC Leawood.

Library of Congress Cataloging-in-Publication Data

Stevenson, James (date)
Oh no, it's Waylon's birthday! / by James Stevenson.
p.   cm.
Summary: Three short stories featuring Waylon
the elephant celebrating his 249th birthday,
Gardner the hippo looking for a quiet
place to sleep, and six penguins walking
on a slippery iceberg.
ISBN 0-688-08235-1.
ISBN 0-688-08236-X (lib. bdg.)
1. Children's stories, American.
[1. Animals—Fiction.
2. Short stories.]   I. Title.
PZ7.S84748Oh 1989   [E]—dc19
88-4574   CIP   AC

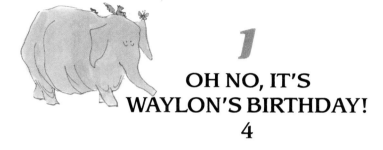

1

OH NO, IT'S WAYLON'S BIRTHDAY!

Dudley, Lucille, and Lewis were playing hide-and-seek when they ran into Waylon. He was looking sad.

"What's the matter, Waylon?" asked Lewis.

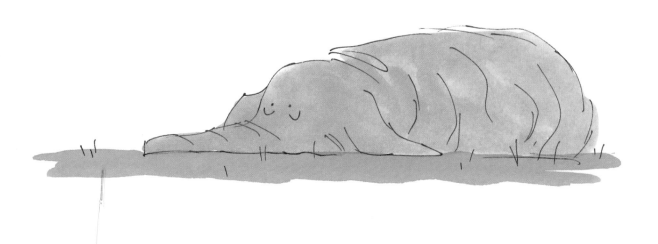

"Next week's my birthday," said Waylon.

"How old will you be?" asked Lucille.

"Two hundred and forty-nine," said Waylon.

"My goodness," said Lucille. "Are you sure you're that old?"

"Elephants never forget," said Waylon.

"What would you like for your birthday?"
  asked Dudley.

"I don't know," said Waylon. "I've already got
  every present there is to get."

"How about a basketball?" said Dudley.

"I was given a basketball in 1910," said Waylon.

"Roller skates?" said Dudley.

"1893," said Waylon.

"Scarf? Mittens? Harmonica?" said Dudley.

"1857, 1882, and 1923," said Waylon.

"Oh," said Dudley.

"Just look at all the birthday stuff in my barn,"
said Waylon. "Under **B** alone I've got boats,
boots, bats, balls, beanbags, banjos,
bathtowels—"
"Dusty in there," said Lewis.

"Maybe a nice birthday cake?" said Lucille.
"How about that?"

"I've had 248 of 'em," said Waylon. "Layer
cakes, sponge cakes, angel food, devil's
food, chocolate…Every kind of icing…
Crowded with candles…"

"Ice cream?" asked Dudley.

"There isn't a flavor I'm not bored with by
now," said Waylon.

"Maybe a party with favors?" Lewis asked.

"I've put on every possible party hat," said
Waylon. "I've popped every party-popper
a person could pop."

"What you want is something different,"
said Lewis. "Am I correct?"

"Darn right," said Waylon. "Different —
  or forget it!"

"Different is difficult," said Lewis.

"Darn right," said Dudley and Lucille.

"We'd better give this some serious
  thought," said Lucille.

"After all," said Dudley, "he's only 249 once."

"Hmmmm," said Lewis.

A week later, on his birthday, Waylon got up and looked around. It was very quiet. There was nobody in sight.

Along came Dudley.
"What's happening?" asked Waylon.
"Nothing in particular," said Dudley. He went on his way.

Lucille fluttered by.

"Where's everybody?" asked Waylon.

"Nowhere special," she said, and flew away.

"This birthday is different, all right," said Waylon. "A little too different."

Waylon decided to take a nap. He fell asleep
and dreamed of birthdays long ago, when
everything was a surprise.

Waylon woke up. Somebody was
whispering in his ear.
It was Lucille.
"What did you say?" asked Waylon.
"Happy birthday, Waylon," whispered Lucille.
"Thank you," said Waylon.

"Here's some ice cream, Waylon,"

whispered Lewis.

"Where?" asked Waylon.

"In this dish,"

Lewis whispered.

"What dish?" asked Waylon.

"In this tiny dish,"

whispered Lewis.

"Why is everybody whispering?" asked Waylon.

"Because this is your smallest and quietest birthday ever,"

whispered Lucille.

"I see," said Waylon.

"Happy birthday, Waylon,"

whispered Dudley.

"Here's your cake!"

" I don't see it," said Waylon.

"Small, isn't it?"

whispered Dudley.

"Make a wish and blow out the candles!"

"Okay," said Waylon. He gave a puff.
Dudley went rolling and tumbling.

"Did all the candles go out?" asked Waylon.
"Let me check," said Dudley. There was a long
  pause.
"Yes," said Dudley. "All 250!"

Then Lewis and Lucille and Dudley sang
"Happy Birthday" to Waylon, and Waylon
took them all for a ride.
"What did you wish, Waylon?" asked Lewis.
"I made a wish about next year's birthday,"
said Waylon. "The big 250th."

"Oh-oh," said Lucille. "Did you wish it
would be *different*?"

"No," said Waylon. "I wished it would
be exactly like this."

2

GARDNER

Gardner kept yawning.

"I really need some sleep," he said.

But the jungle was noisy.

The birds screamed. The lion roared.

The monkeys jumped around, chattering.
"*Could* we have some quiet, please?"
   said Gardner.
"Why?" asked the monkeys. "Is it noisy?"
"It sure is," said Gardner. He walked away
   to the river.

"I'll go all the way to the middle," said Gardner.
He swam out.

"Nobody can bother me here," he said.
He started to fall asleep.

"Hey! No snoring around here!" yelled a frog.
"Sorry," said Gardner. He moved downriver to
a quiet spot and dozed off again.

A flight of cranes landed on Gardner, all
talking at once.

"Excuse me," said Gardner. "I was trying
to sleep—"

"Don't interrupt," said a crane. "We're
having a conversation."

Gardner decided to go underwater.

"Of all the nerve," said a crane.

"Not a polite hippo at all," said another.

Gardner sank to the bottom.

"Perfect," he said, resting in the mud.

"You almost squished me!" said a crab.

"Me, too!" said another.

"Same here!" said a third.

"Didn't mean to," said Gardner.

Suddenly, Gardner was surrounded by fish.
"Get out of the way!" they said. "Do you have
to take up the whole river?"

Gardner tried to get away from the fish and
bumped into three cross turtles.
"Watch it!" said the turtles. "Clumsy fool!"

Gardner rose to the surface and knocked
a crocodile into the air.

"Oops," said Gardner.

"Beat it!" said the crocodile.

Gardner swam as fast as he could toward
the shore.

The cranes were standing in the shallow
water.

"Look out!" cried one. "It's that awful hippo
again!"

"Sorry," said Gardner, tipping over cranes
as he swam. "Sorry..."

At last he reached home.

"Back so soon?" said a monkey.

"I thought you wanted quiet, Gardner," said
a bird.

"I tried quiet," said Gardner. "What I want
now is some good, loud noise."

3

SLIPPERY ICE

It was very cold on the iceberg.

"It's too cold to sit around," said Ralph.

"It's too cold to go swimming," said Alf.

"Let's go for a walk," said Merrill.

"Good idea," said Darryl.

The ice was as slippery as glass.

It was hard to walk without falling down.

Ralph and Alf and Merrill and Darryl held
onto each other.

"Oh-oh," said Darryl. "Here comes Cheryl!"

"You'll crash into us!" said Merrill.

"Stop!" said Darryl.

"Stop!" said Alf.

"How?" said Cheryl.

Cheryl crashed into Darryl.

Darryl crashed into Merrill.

Merrill crashed into Alf.

Alf crashed into Ralph.

"Hey!" said Ralph.

"Where are you going, Ralph?" called Alf.

"I have no idea," called Ralph.

"Be careful," called Darryl.

"Thanks," said Ralph.

"Try to turn, Ralph!" called Alf.

"I'm trying," called Ralph.

"Ralph's turning," said Alf.

"Now he's coming back," said Merrill.

"Look out!" said Darryl.

"Stop, Ralph!" called Alf.

THUMP!

"I'm back," said Ralph.

"We know," said Alf.

"Oh-oh," said Cheryl.

"What now?" said Darryl.

"Here comes Beryl," said Cheryl.

"Maybe she'll miss us," said Darryl.

"I hope so," said Cheryl.

"Somebody grab my wing!" said Beryl.

"Not me!" said Cheryl.

"Or me!" said Darryl.

"Here!" said Ralph. "I'll help you."

"Oh-oh!" said everybody.

They flew across the ice.

At last they began to slow down.

But the end of the iceberg was just ahead.

They came to a stop at the very edge of the ice.

"That was close," said Ralph.

"We almost fell in," said Alf. "And it looks
  awfully cold."

"Where's Beryl?" said Cheryl.

"Here I am!" said Beryl.

"Sorry," said Beryl. "It was slippery."

"We know," said Darryl.

"It's not so cold," said Cheryl.

"Once you get in," said the others.

"That's what I mean," said Cheryl,
 and they all went for a swim.